D1144752

S412

PRINCE JAKE

JAKE

He's the Prince of Pranks!

Sticky Gum Fun

FOR JACK MONGREDIEN,
WITH LOTS OF LOVE
S.M.

FOR MY MUM, CATHERINE
M.B.

ORCHARD BOOKS
338 Euston Road, London NW1 3BH
Orchard Books Australia
Level 17/205 Kent St, Sydney, NSW 2000

First published in 2008 by Orchard Books
First paperback publication in 2009
Text © Sue Mongredien 2008
Illustrations © Mark Beech 2008

The rights of Sue Mongredien to be identified as the author
and Mark Beech to be identified as the illustrator of this work
have been asserted by them in accordance with
the Copyright, Designs and Patents Act, 1988.
A CIP catalogue record for this book is available from the British Library.

ISBN HB 978 1 40830 276 7
ISBN PB 978 1 84616 618 1

1 3 5 7 9 10 8 6 4 2

Printed in Great Britain by
CPI Antony Rowe, Chippenham, Wiltshire

Orchard Books is a division of Hachette Children's Books
an Hachette Livre UK company.
www.hachettelivre.co.uk

He's the Prince of Pranks!

PRINCE JAKE

Sticky Gum Fun

SUE MONGREDIEN ♛ MARK BEECH

ORCHARD BOOKS

CHAPTER ONE

"Jacob Leopold Gregorio the Fourth – I want a word with you, son!"

Prince Jake looked up from his gold-plated bowl of crownflakes to see the King of Morania entering the banqueting hall. Uh-oh. His dad never used his full name unless he was in big trouble. What had he done wrong now?

"Yes, Dad?" Jake asked. He quickly tried to think what it might be. OK,

so he'd swiped a whole bottle of
the Queen's poshest bubble bath
yesterday – but it *had* been an
emergency. He'd only been trying to
make the dog, Nervous Rex, smell nicer
after Jake had taken him swimming in
the moat. It wasn't Jake's fault that Rex
hadn't liked his bath very much, and
had left a trail of bubbles all over the
west wing of the palace!

"What's Boy Wonder been up to now,
then?" Princess Petunia, Jake's big
sister, asked sarcastically. She arched
a perfectly plucked eyebrow. "Maybe
it's time to send him to the dungeon
for a few weeks. The peace and quiet
would be bliss!"

Jake flicked a soggy crownflake at
Petunia as she turned to smirk at their
dad. Result! It landed straight in her
hair without her even noticing.

King Nicholas sat down opposite Jake at the royal breakfast table. He planted his great elbows either side of his cereal bowl. "Jake, do you know anything about the bubble gum I found on my throne last night?" he asked, his dark eyes fixed on his son.

"Bubble gum?" Jake echoed innocently. Ahh. So that was what this was all about.

"Yes, bubble gum!" the King spluttered.

"Because I sat right in it! At the Moranian Fisherwomen's Gala Dinner last night!"

"The Moranian what?" Jake repeated, trying not to snigger.

Queen Caroline put down her tea cup and frowned at her eldest son. "It's not funny, Jake. Your father could hardly stand up, he was so firmly stuck to the throne."

"And when I did finally manage to unstick myself, there was a dreadful squelch, and all of the wretched fisherwomen started giggling at me," the King said sternly. "Cackling, they were, like a load of fishwives."

"They *were* fishwives," Queen Caroline reminded him.

"Sorry, Dad," Jake mumbled, shovelling in more crownflakes. "I must have… um…dropped it."

Jake crossed his fingers under the table. He couldn't tell his parents why he'd *really* been using the sticky gum on his dad's throne. It wasn't as if he'd knocked that gold knobble off it with his Frisbee on purpose!

"Hmph," King Nicholas rumbled. "Well, you can show me how sorry you are by cleaning the suits of armour this morning. Our guests will want to see them later, when we show them around the castle." He opened his newspaper with a flourish.

"But—" Jake protested.

"No buts," the Queen said, giving Jake one of her looks. "Now, children," she went on, before he could say anything else, "I need you all to be on your best behaviour today. The royal family of Pratzia are arriving later this morning, and they'll be staying with us for a few days. It seems that their castle has a rather nasty rat

10

infestation. Most unfortunate." Jake noticed her give a little sigh as she glanced out of the window at her beloved flowering borders. He knew she'd much rather be up to her royal elbows in mulch and seedlings than entertaining visitors.

Princess Petunia's mouth opened and shut a few times. "Did you just say the royal family of *Pratzia*?" she asked breathlessly. "Did you really just say—?"

"Yes, dear, I did," the Queen said, briskly. "And please don't leave your mouth hanging open like that. If any of the Moranian fisherwomen are still lurking around, they'll think you're one of their prize haddocks."

Petunia's eyes were shining. "So Prince Rupert's going to be here?" she asked. "Actually staying here, in our castle?"

"Yes, dear," the Queen said. "The whole family are coming."

Princess Petunia jumped to her feet with a most un-princess-like squawk. "Why didn't you tell me before? I've got to wash my hair and paint my nails and get my tiaras polished, like, now!" she wailed, bolting out of the banqueting hall in a blur of golden hair and pinkness.

Jake rolled his eyes at his brother, Prince Ned. "Perfect Petunia's got it bad," he hissed. "There are loads of pictures of the Pratzian prince on her bedroom wall, aren't there?"

"What's got into that girl?" Queen Caroline sighed, watching Petunia go. "Still, she does have a point. We all need to look respectable for the Pratzians. They're very rich and very glamorous." She looked her sons up and down with a rather disapproving expression. "Superhero costumes and jeans are absolutely forbidden while the Pratzians are here.

We can't have them thinking they're staying in a youth hostel."

Jake looked down at his favourite tatty jeans, complete with grass stains and large rips in the knees, and sighed.

Prince Ned looked down at his Spider-Man costume, and sighed too. "Not even my Spider-Man mask?" he tried.

The Queen shook her head. "Not even your Spider-Man *pants*," she said. "I will ask Boris to find something suitable for you both to wear instead."

Jake groaned as his mum swished out of the room. "Something suitable" meant one of his awful smart suits. Yuck! Sometimes he hated being a prince!

There was a great rustling sound then, and King Nicholas's head popped up above his newspaper. "By the way, son," he said in a low voice, "I meant to ask – what flavour was that bubble gum on my throne? It smelled really good."

"Strawbalicious," Jake replied. He delved into his pocket and pulled out a silver packet. "Do you want some? I've got a bit left. It's super-sticky."

The King's arm shot over his newspaper and reached for the gum. A smile spread across his face as he chewed. "Boris?" he called to the butler, who'd just come in. "Get me and the boys two hundred boxes of this Strawbalicious gum, please. Don't

forget to tell them it's for His Majesty
the King!" Then he turned back to Jake
with a stern face. "But no more on my
throne – or else!"

Jake grinned. "OK, Dad," he said. Two
hundred boxes of gum – cool! Sometimes
he loved being a prince. "You're the boss."

King Nicholas sat up straighter in his
chair and puffed out his chest. "I am
indeed, son," he said. "I am indeed."

CHAPTER TWO

"Here's your silver polish, and some rags,"
said Mrs Pinny, the royal housekeeper,
a little while later. "And don't forget to
wear an apron, will you? Otherwise
you'll get filthy." She paused and looked
disdainfully at Jake's grubby T-shirt.
"Mind you, you couldn't get *much* dirtier
than you already are…but never mind."

"Thanks, Mrs Pinny," Jake said dolefully,
as she bundled the cleaning things into

his arms. At the top of the pile sat a pink, frilly apron, and he scowled. He was definitely not wearing *that*!

Jake gazed at all the rusty suits of armour in front of him with a heavy heart. This lot was going to take him ages! It was so unfair! Wasn't it supposed to be a princely perk that royal families didn't have to do any chores? Even two hundred boxes of gum wasn't worth this!

"Now then," Mrs Pinny muttered to herself as she headed out of the room. "Beds to be made, tapestries to be brushed, royal helicopter to be polished…"

Jake set to work on his first suit of armour. He swept off all the cobwebs. He scraped away all the rust. Then he smeared on the smelly silver polish and rubbed and rubbed until his arms ached.

Prince Ned appeared in the doorway just as Jake was finishing his sixth silver suit. Ned was looking very uncomfortable in his slightly too-big outfit. "They're here," he said mournfully, looking down and scuffing a polished shoe along the floor. "Mum says we've got to go and bow and stuff." Then Ned looked up and burst out laughing.

"What?" Jake asked, turning red. He had polish on his nose, cobwebs in his

hair…oh, and a frilly pink apron tied
around his middle. Well, he didn't want
to ruin his favourite jeans with rust
streaks, did he?

Mrs Pinny bustled back into the armour room just then, and clapped a hand to her mouth at the sight of Jake. It was obvious she was trying hard to hold back her giggles. "Pink is ever so *you*, Master Jake," she tittered, "but it's probably best if you change out of that frilly little number before you greet the visitors, don't you think?" She started scrubbing at Jake's face with a large flowery handkerchief. "Just look at the state of you," she tutted. "You can't meet the Pratzians like this. You simply can't. Your poor mum will have a fit!"

A grin slid over Jake's face. Excellent! Did that mean he was going to get out of the posh lunch the Queen had arranged for them all?

"So I'll take you to your room and get you cleaned up at once," Mrs Pinny went on bossily. "Boris has picked out a smashing suit for you. Lovely, it is, a sort of mushy-pea green colour. Ever so stylish! Run along now, Prince Ned, there's a poppet. Prince Jake – you're coming with me."

Jake groaned as Mrs Pinny hustled him out of the armour room and along the corridor. This day was turning into a right royal write-off!

One hot shower, one close encounter with the comb and a wrestling match with his collar and tie later, Prince Jake was shooed along by Boris to meet the Pratzians. His shirt itched, his tie was half-strangling him, and his smart shoes pinched his toes. Why couldn't princes wear what they wanted, anyway? Someone should pass a law about it, in Jake's opinion.

"Better late than never," the Queen said, as Jake entered the grand hall. She looked him up and down quickly, and an expression of relief came over her face.

"Scrubbed up nicely, Jakey, well done," she said in a low voice, before ushering him over to a fat man in a tight suit with what looked suspiciously like a toupee on his head, a tall woman with no chin and their smirking, oily-haired son. They were all sitting on the best red sofa, which was reserved for only the most important bottoms. Jake had certainly never been allowed to put *his* princely bottom anywhere near it.

King Nicholas came over and put a hand on Jake's shoulder. "King Oliver, Queen Millie and Prince Rupert, I'd like you to meet my eldest son, Prince Jake," he said.

"All right?" Jake asked, then blushed. "I mean, hello. Nice to meet you."

The fat man in the tight suit – King Oliver – got to his feet and began pumping Jake's hand up and down. "Jake, eh?" he

wheezed. "By gum, you're a chip off the old block, eh! I was just talking about golf with your father. We're going to take to the royal course after lunch for a few holes. Like golf, do you, eh?"

Jake had only ever played golf once, and the only hole he'd made had been the one in the stained glass window in the oldest part of the castle. "Well, my tutor *did* say I was a smashing player," he replied carefully, not daring to look at his parents.

"Excellent, excellent," cried King Oliver. "Rupert here is a splendid player, too. Better than any other fifteen-year-old in Pratzia, he tells me, by gum. So that'll make a four. Good-o!" He finally released Jake's hand, which felt as if all the blood had been squeezed out of it.

Rupert looked down at Jake, his mouth curled in a sneer.

Jake scowled back, trying not to scrunch his hands up into fists.

Then there came a slight cough from King Oliver's left. Princess Petunia was blushing furiously. "Um…your Highness, I'd love to join you, too, if I may," she said politely. "I'm quite partial to a bit of golf myself, and…" She batted her eyelashes, and blushed an even deeper crimson. "And I'd simply love to see how well Prince Rupert can play."

Queen Millie snickered behind a skinny hand. "But you're a *girl!*" she said.

King Oliver's eyebrows had shot right into his hairline. "By gum, Princess, dear me, no!" he said. He was shaking his round, red ball of a head so fast that Jake was sure he spotted the toupee swivel. "I don't think so!"

"She's much better than I am," Jake said quickly, hoping to wriggle out of having to play himself.

27

"She certainly is," Queen Caroline agreed, her eyes flicking up to the beautiful rose window above them.

"My handicap is four," Petunia added. "And I *did* win the Teen Princess Golf Tournament last year."

Queen Millie gave a laugh like a hysterical horse and her husband joined in wheezily. Jake was half expecting King Oliver's fat head to deflate, with all the wheezing he was doing. And surely that toupee was about to fly off at any second!

"I really don't think so, sweetheart," Prince Rupert said smoothly. "The golf course is no place for a girl!"

Princess Petunia's cheeks flamed and she looked down at the floor, crushed. Jake thought he could see her eyes welling up, under all that shiny hair. He didn't often feel sorry for his sister, but right now he did. Mind you, Jake felt sorry for himself, too. He'd rather be scrubbing more suits of armour than have to suffer golf with the Pratzians!

The Queen put a calming hand on her daughter's arm and smiled brightly around the room. "I do believe lunch will be served any moment now," she said. She nodded meaningfully at Boris, who hurried out of the door. "Shall we make our way to the banqueting hall?"

"That would be lovely," said Queen Millie, primly.

Prince Jake pulled a face at Ned as they followed the royal visitors into the banqueting hall. Lovely? No chance. With the royal prats staying, Jake was certain he was in for a most *un*-lovely few days!

CHAPTER THREE

"So, Rupert, what else do you like doing besides golf?" Queen Caroline asked politely as they tucked into their smoked salmon starter.

Prince Rupert smiled a tight little smile as if he were pleased to have been asked. "I'm captain of the Pratzian polo team," he drawled. "I broke the national swimming record for my freestyle 100 metres, and I'm also the undefeated

Pratzian tennis champion." He flicked back his oily hair, and smirked. "Of course, I'm extremely intelligent, too. In fact, I…"

Prince Jake glanced over at his sister, who seemed rapt over Rupert's every word, a soppy smile on her face. Couldn't she *see* that he was an utter creep and a show-off?

"And it's my firm belief that all young princes should set an example to their country," Prince Rupert said smugly. "Not

just in sport and intelligence, but in fashion and hair care, too. It's so important!"

Jake's knife skidded on his plate, and a pea shot across the table. It flew right up over the royal serving dishes, pinged off Prince Rupert's rather large nose and landed in his glass of water.

"I say!" Rupert snorted indignantly.

"Manners!" hissed Queen Caroline.

"It was an accident!" Jake said, looking as innocent as he possibly could.

He pressed his lips together to stop himself laughing out loud at the sight of the pea bobbing about in Prince Rupert's drink. Talk about a hole-in-one!

Prince Ned giggled into his serviette, and King Nicholas shot them both a warning look. Queen Millie looked as if she'd been drinking lemon juice through a straw.

"Please excuse my brothers, Rupert," Princess Petunia said, using a solid silver teaspoon to fish the pea from Rupert's drink. She smiled sweetly at him, and her cheeks dimpled. "I do hope for their sakes that one day they'll grow up to be just as wonderful and well-mannered as you."

Jake couldn't help letting out a snort. In his worst nightmares! What planet was his sister on, anyway?

Queen Caroline leaned over and caught Jake's eye. "Any more bad behaviour from you and you'll be banned from the game of golf," she said. And then, when nobody was looking, Jake was sure his mum gave Petunia the tiniest little wink.

Jake stared at her, puzzled. Had he imagined it?

His mum tipped her head ever so slightly in Petunia's direction, then looked meaningfully at Jake. "I'm sure you wouldn't want your sister to take your place in the golf by being naughty, Jake, would you?" she said.

Jake grinned. He *hadn't* imagined the wink. Good old Mum! She'd just given him a perfect golf get-out!

"Rupert, sweetie, what were you saying before you were interrupted?" Queen Millie twittered, her face slightly less sour. "Something about your being captain of the Pratzian chess team, wasn't it?"

"Chess team, tennis team… Gosh, actually, I'm pretty much captain of everything," Rupert boasted, with another toss of his hair. "In fact, I've got some photos in my pocket that I'm sure you'd all love to see." He pulled out a thick wedge of glossy prints and started leafing through them. "Here's one of me reciting my prize-winning poem *A Prince's Pride* at the Pratzian Festival – just look at the crowd! And here's one of me with the wild boar I caught single-handedly in the mountains. And here's another of…"

Jake couldn't bear it any more. Wild boar? Wild *bore*, more like! The only prize Prince Rupert deserved was one for Show-Off of the Century. Jake had to shut him up, and fast!

Jake leaned across the table, reaching to get the pepper and...whoops! He knocked his blackcurrant drink all over Prince Rupert, and all over Prince Rupert's photos. "Oh dear!" he said, trying to sound surprised.

"Jake!" his mother shouted. "You're so clumsy! Right – I did warn you. Petunia, you can take Jake's place on the golf course. And no quibbling!"

King Oliver opened his mouth to say something – something about girls on golf courses, no doubt – but Queen Caroline was looking so fierce that he seemed to think better of it. He popped in a roast potato instead and chewed it thoughtfully.

"Really, Mum?" beamed Petunia, her eyes lighting up. "Great!"

Jake cast his eyes down as one of the waiters fussed over Prince Rupert, mopped him dry, and then led him off to find a pair of clean trousers. Jake sat very still, and tried to look as repentant as possible. Inside, though, he was jumping up and down, punching the air. A purple-stained,

wet-trousered Rupert, and no golf!
YESSSS! Queen Millie had been right:
lunch had turned out to be quite lovely
after all.

CHAPTER FOUR

After lunch, the golf party left for their game, and Queen Caroline and Queen Millie went horse-riding.

While their parents were both out, Prince Jake and Prince Ned decided to go skateboarding around the castle. Jake had worked out that if the drawbridge was at a certain angle, you could use it as a brilliant skateboarding ramp. If you built up enough speed as you came out of the

great hall, and up the sloping drawbridge,
you could go flying over the moat.
Unfortunately, if the drawbridge was at
the *wrong* angle, you tended to go flying
into the moat.

Of course, that didn't worry Jake and
Ned. Quite the opposite! It was such a hot
day that having the odd clump of
pondweed dripping around one's neck was
strangely refreshing. Nervous Rex, the
dog, seemed to agree. He was having

a great time splashing about in the moat, barking at all the ducks and getting muddier by the minute.

"Prince Rupert is such a show-off," Jake complained as he clambered out of the moat for the fourth time. "I can't believe Petunia is potty enough to fancy *him*."

Prince Ned wiped some frogspawn out of his hair as they sat on the grassy bank. "Did you see the way she was batting her eyelashes at him all through lunch?" he said. "After he was so mean to her about the golf and everything."

Jake spun the wheels on his skateboard. "*We're* the only ones who are allowed to be mean to her," he agreed. "He was totally out of order."

Just then the drawbridge creaked down to its resting place, and Boris the butler walked over it. His eyebrows lifted slightly at the sight of the Princes' weed-splattered

shirts, their muddy trousers and their
dripping wet hair, but if he was surprised
by their appearance, he didn't say so. He
coughed delicately to get their attention.
"Your Highnesses, just to let you know
that the Queen has returned from her
riding trip," he said. "And the owner of
the golf lodge phoned to say that the King
and his guests are on their way back from
the game." Jake was sure he could see
a smile twitching at the corners of Boris's
mouth. "I believe Princess Petunia had an
excellent round."

"Better than rotten Rupert?" Jake asked
hopefully, his fingers crossed.

Boris nodded. "I do believe so," he
replied, to Jake and Ned's cheers. Then he
glanced at his watch, and back at the
Princes. "Perhaps I could help you...
ahem...tidy yourselves up before anyone
else sees you?" he offered.

Jake looked at his brother's bedraggled
appearance, then caught sight of his tie
floating among the bulrushes down in the
moat. He nodded reluctantly. "It's
probably a good idea," he said with
a small sigh. He patted his skateboard,
wondering if he could try that triple
jump back-spin one more time. He so
wanted to get it right just once, without
being dunked...

"Your gum has arrived," Boris put in at that moment. "All two hundred boxes of it. It's waiting for you in your bedroom. The smell of strawberries is quite overwhelming," he added faintly.

"Brilliant," Jake said, jumping to his feet at once. "Come on, Ned. Thanks, Boris!"

In clean clothes once more, and with all traces of moat-life well and truly scrubbed away, Jake and Ned trooped towards the garden. According to Boris, Queen Caroline had arranged a game of croquet to entertain the royal guests.

Jake and his brother were just passing the suite of rooms where Rupert and his parents were staying, when a voice floated through the door.

"Cheating, she was. Cheating! She must have been. How else could a girl – a mere *girl* – have beaten me?"

Jake stopped in his tracks and glanced at Ned. It was Rupert!

"What a bad loser," Ned muttered indignantly.

"What a loser, full stop," Jake agreed.

Jake and Ned hid behind a large marble statue of their dad to listen.

"Her Royal Highness Princess Petunia *is* very good at golf," they heard Alex, the assistant butler, say loyally. There was a pause. "Perhaps there was a problem with your clubs, your Highness."

47

"Must have been. Must have been!" came Prince Rupert's shrill reply. "Should have known the golfing facilities would be shabby here. This whole place is a dump! You should see our castle in Pratzia. Now *that's* fit for a king, and no mistake. It's twice as big and twice as beautiful as the Moranian morons' castle, believe me."

Jake could feel his fists clenching again as he listened to Prince Rupert's boasting. "I've had enough! We've *got* to do something to shut him up," he muttered to Ned behind his dad's royal behind. "But what?"

CHAPTER FIVE

Jake popped in some Strawbalicious gum to help himself think. He thought and thought as he walked along the royal hall, through the rose garden, past the tennis courts and all the way down to the croquet lawn.

"Gum *out*, please," Queen Caroline hissed as he went to get his mallet.

He thought hard as Princess Petunia racked up the highest croquet score, and harder still as Prince Rupert turned puce with bitterness.

Jake thought even harder as Prince Rupert announced that croquet was for silly girlies and that the Moranians couldn't play proper sports anyway, not like the Pratzians.

And he was still thinking when King Nicholas said, rather curtly, that he distinctly remembered the Moranian football team beating the Pratzians 2–1 just last week, actually. "And well done anyway, Petunia," the King added pointedly. "A well-deserved croquet victory there, I think!" He shot a look at Rupert before turning back to his daughter. "You certainly showed that you are a better croquet player than *any* of us."

"Thanks, Daddy," Petunia said, looking flushed and pleased. She smiled over at Rupert, obviously hoping that he too would give her a word of praise, but he

just glared at her and kicked the croquet
ball into the bushes.

"Mind my delphiniums!" Queen
Caroline cried in anguish.

King Nicholas had to rush his wife off
to prepare for dinner before she lost her
temper. It was quite clear to Jake that
everyone was sick of Prince Rupert!

Jake popped in another piece of
Strawbalicious as he went upstairs to get
dressed for dinner. *Mmm, super-sticky!*
he thought, chewing hard. And then, in

the very next second, he had an idea.
A brain-bogglingly brilliant idea!

Jake ran at once to Prince Ned's
bedroom. "Do me a favour?" he asked,
thrusting the gum packet into his
brother's hand. "Start chewing up some
of this lot. Only don't throw it away.
Chew up as many pieces as you can and
then, when they're good and sticky, save
them for me, OK?"

"Why?" Prince Ned asked, obediently
unwrapping a piece of gum and putting it
in his mouth.

"I've got a plan," Jake replied with a grin. "And I'll be right back."

Jake sprinted down to the armour room, which was still unlocked. Then, very carefully, he picked up one of the newly cleaned suits of armour and dragged it back upstairs. He was heading rather slowly up the corridor when he saw Alex.

"Goodness! Do you want a hand with that?" Alex asked, rushing over at once.

"Please," Jake said. "Actually, I was hoping you could help me with something else, too. Just a little surprise for Prince Rupert."

Alex's eyes met Jake's across the armour as they carried it between them. "Of course, your Highness," Alex said. "Whatever you want."

"Good," replied Jake, with a mischievous smile. "I was hoping you'd say that."

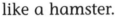

Alex helped Jake carry the armour all the way into Ned's bedroom, where Prince Ned greeted them with cheeks like a hamster.

"Ibe onkurgh by hunhurgh bee," he said, between chomps.

"Onto your hundredth piece? Brilliant," Jake said. "Although you didn't have to keep it *all* in your mouth at the same time!"

Ned's swollen cheeks deflated as he

removed the large pink ball of chewed gum
from his mouth and passed it to Jake.
"Super-sticky," he declared.

"Good job," said Jake, sitting down next
to him. He turned the silver helmet from
the suit of armour upside down on his lap
and started pressing the pink bubble gum
inside it. He made sure there was gum all
around the inside edge of the helmet,
and, most importantly, a large lump of it
inside the topmost point.

Alex watched with interest. "And this is
for...?" he asked, wonderingly.

Jake winked. "For Prince Charming
himself, of course," he said with a grin.
"Your friend and mine – Loopy Rupe. You
see, tonight's dinner is going to be fancy
dress – and this is Rupert's costume,
right here."

"Is it *really* fancy dress?" Ned asked
eagerly. "Brilliant! I'm going to be Batman."

Jake shook his head. "Sorry, mate, no," he said. "It's only fancy dress for Prince Rupert – although *he* won't know that, of course. There!" He stuck the last lump of bubble gum in place and turned the helmet the right way up. "This is where you come in, Alex," he said, looking at the butler with pleading eyes.

"I had a feeling it might be," Alex replied. He took the helmet gingerly. "Give me my orders, your Highness," he said with a grin.

CHAPTER SIX

Jake got ready for dinner in super-quick
time to give him a chance for a spot of
sneaky eavesdropping outside Prince
Rupert's room.

"Fancy dress?" Prince Rupert was saying
suspiciously when Jake crept up to listen
at the keyhole. "Nobody told *me* it was
going to be fancy dress."

"I have your costume right here," Jake
heard Alex say amidst clanking sounds.

Jake guessed that Alex was holding up the
suit of armour, and crossed his fingers.
Please let Rupert fall for this one, he
prayed. Please!

"Hmph," he heard Prince Rupert mutter.
"Fancy dress is for kids. I'm sure Princess
Fluffy and her half-witted oiks of brothers
love that sort of thing, but for a mature,
sophisticated prince like me... I'll probably
just put on a crown and go as a king."

Jake bit his lip. This was all about to go
wrong. He *had* to do something!

"Hello?" he said brightly, putting his
head around the door. "Sorry to interrupt,
Prince Rupert, but I couldn't help
overhearing. If you don't want to wear
the armour, then I will. Did you know
it's actually the very suit of armour that
King Samuel wore as he defeated the
Vulcranians in battle, over eight hundred
years ago?"

Prince Rupert's eyes popped. "Really?" he asked. "Gosh."

Jake nodded. "The thing is, it's the only outfit we've got in your size. So if you don't want to wear it..." He pretended to consider. "I suppose you could always borrow one of my mum's ballgowns and go dressed as a princess instead." He stretched out a hand for the armour. "Anyway, if you're not going to wear it, that means I can, right?"

Prince Rupert stepped forwards and
snatched the suit of armour from Alex.
"Wrong!" he said. "Find your own
costume, sunshine, this one's got *my* name
on it." He clutched it protectively. "Help
me put this on, will you?" he asked Alex.
"Quickly now! I mustn't be late for
Mummy and Daddy!"

Jake tried not to smirk as Rupert slid his arms into the silver sleeves. Job done. Job *well* done! "Oh, and don't forget the helmet, will you?" he added casually as he turned to leave the room. "That's the most important bit of all."

A little while later, Jake sat down to dinner in the banqueting hall. Everyone was dressed to impress. King Nicholas and King Oliver were both in their best suits. The two Queens wore silk dresses and dripped with diamonds. Petunia was looking perfectly polished in a flouncy pink ballgown, while Jake and Ned wriggled uncomfortably in their smart trousers and shirts that still felt warm from the iron.

"Dear me, where's Rupert got to, I wonder?" Queen Millie said, glancing down at her watch. "Probably doing his hair again," she mused. "It does tend to take him a while, you see. All that gel and spray he puts on."

61

"Mousse too, don't forget," King Oliver added, glancing at his reflection in the shining silver soup tureen. He patted his own hair rather wistfully, Jake couldn't help noticing.

"And he's always borrowing my hair straighteners," Queen Millie said. "I have told him. Rupert, I've said, it'll all fall out if you keep putting so much stuff on it. But will he listen? No. Never listens to me." She caught herself suddenly and

put on a bright smile. "Still – all that preening is worth it, eh? He does always look so handsome."

"He does," Petunia agreed.

Queen Millie gave her a gracious smile. "Oh, he's going to make the most wonderful King some…"

Clank, clank, clank.

Queen Millie stopped abruptly. "Whatever was *that*?" she asked.

The clanking sound was getting nearer.

63

CLANK. CLANK. CLANK.

The door swung open and a gasp went up as an armoured figure staggered in, his silver helmet gleaming under the chandelier.

"What on earth…? What's going on?" King Nicholas boomed.

CLANK! CLANK! CLANK!

Jake pressed his lips together to stop himself from laughing out loud as Prince Rupert stumbled further into the room – and then clumsily lurched straight into the dining table!

CRASH! There went the best glass goblets!

SMASH! There went Prince Rupert, toppling into the soup tureen!

SPLASH! There went the soup, splattering all over Princess Petunia!

"Oh!" gasped Petunia, who was covered in green soup. (Luckily, it was the posh cold kind, and not hot at all.) "My *hair*!"

"Boris, kindly remove this oaf from our table at once!" thundered Queen Caroline.

"Who *is* this idiot knight?" screeched Queen Millie.

"Sorry, Mummy," the idiot knight said pathetically. He staggered to his feet, knocking King Oliver flying from his chair as he did so. A small brown furry thing went whizzing through the air...straight into what was left of the soup! *So it had been a toupee*, thought Jake with a chuckle ...only it was a soggy green one now.

"By gum!" King Oliver gasped from where he'd landed on the floor. The shining bald patch on his round red head looked just like a sunrise. "Is that *you*, Rupert? What on *earth* are you doing?"

CHAPTER SEVEN

Rupert's helmet creaked as he turned to look around the table. "But I thought it was fancy dress!" he spluttered. Then he lifted up the visor and glared accusingly at Jake. "You said…"

Prince Jake smiled as nicely as he knew how. "My mistake," he said. "I got mixed up. It happens to us half-witted oiks all the time."

Prince Rupert snarled a horrible snarl.

"You were all in it together, weren't you?"
he growled. "You stupid little Princes and
your simpering sister!"

"I'll give you simpering sister!" retorted
Princess Petunia hotly, throwing the
soup-sodden toupee at him. "How dare
you speak to me like that, you...you...
metal-headed buffoon!"

"That's quite enough!" Queen Caroline said icily. Jake could feel her eyes boring into him, and he stared down at his plate as if it was the most interesting thing in the world. "Petunia – sit down. Jake – I shall have words with you later."

"You'd better sit down, too, Rupert, and take off your helmet," Queen Millie snapped. "We've all been waiting for you."

"Sorry, Mum," Rupert said, clanking his way awkwardly to his seat. "It's just...oof!...quite difficult to walk in this." He sat down and reached up to take off his helmet.

Jake held his breath.

"I can't seem to..." Rupert muttered. He heaved helplessly at the helmet. "It won't...I can't get it off!"

Princess Petunia giggled, and hurriedly turned it into a cough. Now she was

looking at Prince Rupert with all the scorn
he deserved, Jake noticed with glee.

"Rupert!" Queen Millie said in a sharp
voice. "Stop messing about. Now take off
that helmet *this minute!*"

Rupert's bottom lip quivered above
his chin-rest and he tugged on the
helmet again.

"By gum, lad," King Oliver said crossly.
"Let me." He strode over to his son, took
hold of the helmet with both hands and
heaved.

There was a tremendous ripping sound…
and a squeal of agony from Prince Rupert.
"My hair! Daddy, my hair!"

"There!" said King Oliver triumphantly
as the helmet came away.

A shocked silence fell as everyone stared
at Prince Rupert. There were great clumps
of pink in his precious floppy hair…or
rather, what was left of it.

"Rupert! What *have* you done?" Queen Millie shrieked. "I told you not to put so much spray in it – and now look what's happened!"

"Must have reacted with the silver polish, ma'am," Boris said smoothly. He picked up the helmet from where King Oliver had dropped it on the floor and tucked it behind his back. "I've heard that can happen. The only thing to do is to cut the whole lot off, I'm afraid."

"Hair today, gone tomorrow," Jake put in helpfully.

"It'll be a close shave," Ned added, with a low snigger.

"Like father, like son," Petunia giggled, with an eye on King Oliver's shining bald patch. She shook out her own soup-green locks, accidentally-on-purpose spattering Rupert in the face. "Definitely a bad *heir* day, if you ask me," she added sweetly.

The pungent aroma of strawberries came drifting through the air just then, and King Nicholas sniffed in recognition. Then his eyes widened and he turned to look at Jake.

Uh-oh. Sussed by his dad! Jake braced himself for the worst punishment of his life...

"It's a dreadful thing, helmet hair," King Nicholas said sympathetically to the

Pratzians. "My condolences. Don't worry, Rupert, I'll personally make sure my barber sorts you out, first thing in the morning. Now, if someone could bring us some fresh soup please, we really should start our meal..."

Jake's mouth fell open as the waiters bustled around them with fresh soup and bread. Had he *really* got away with that? Talk about a right royal result!

Jake couldn't help a wicked grin as he tucked into his food. Having the Pratzians to stay had certainly been a *hair-raising* experience so far – but, as King Oliver would say, by gum, he'd had some princely fun, too! Now…what might he get up to tomorrow? He glanced over at Prince Rupert, who was still looking very hot and bothered at the far end of the table. Maybe a spot of drawbridge skateboarding would be just the thing to cool Prince Rupert down…

LOOK OUT FOR MORE
RIGHT ROYAL LAUGHS WITH

Sticky Gum Fun
978 1 40830 276 7   £8.99

It's Snow Joke!
978 1 40830 277 4   £8.99

Dungeon of Doom
978 1 40830 280 4   £8.99

Knighty-Knight
978 1 40830 281 1   £8.99

Monster Madness
978 1 40830 278 1   £8.99

Swordfights and Slimeballs!
978 1 40830 279 8   £8.99

Here's a taster of

It's Snow Joke!

Splat!

"Gotcha!" Prince Jake guffawed with laughter as his snowball whacked right into his little brother's shoulder.

"Oi!" yelped Prince Ned, fumbling to make his own snowball. And then, seconds later…

Wheeeeee!

Ned had hurled his snowball straight back at Jake, who ducked, still laughing helplessly.

He turned his head to see it thwack against the castle wall and shatter onto the frozen moat behind him.

Jake reached down to scoop up a fresh handful of snow and pack together another freezing missile. The powdery snow squeaked under his gloved fingers, and he grinned broadly. How he loved winter! Snow, sledging, Christmas, school holidays…

"Aim…FIRE!" he yelled, sending the snowball whizzing through the crisp winter air in his brother's direction.

SPLAT!

"Oh, yes!" he chortled as it landed right on Ned's bobble hat, sending it skewing sideways over his eyes. "Bullseye! The hotshot prince hits the target yet again, as he…aargggh!"

A return snowball hit him square in the chest, thumping against his coat. "Right," he said, "like that, is it?"

For the next few minutes, the two princes flung snowballs back and forth, laughing and panting breathlessly. They were in the snow-covered formal gardens just outside the castle where they lived with their parents, the King and Queen of Morania, and their older sister, Princess Petunia. It wasn't long before both boys were covered in snow, and their toes were starting to go numb inside their wellies. Then, just as Prince Jake had packed together a truly awesome snowball, Ned started waving his arms, an urgent expression on his face. "Over there!" he called in a low voice. "New target sighted!"

Jake turned to look where Ned was pointing – and grinned. Ahh, perfect. Absolutely perfect! There was Princess Petunia crossing the drawbridge, on her way out of the castle. No better target in the world for the fantastic snowball Jake had just made!

He gave it a last bit of patting and shaping, making sure that all the snow was pressed in, and every curve was smooth. It was a beauty!

PICK UP A COPY OF

It's Snow JoKe!

TO FIND OUT WHAT HAPPENS NEXT!